THIS WALKER BOOK BELONGS TO:

For Sally and Wembury Beach,
and to Peter and Margaret Bryan,
Karen, Jacqui and Alison,
with love

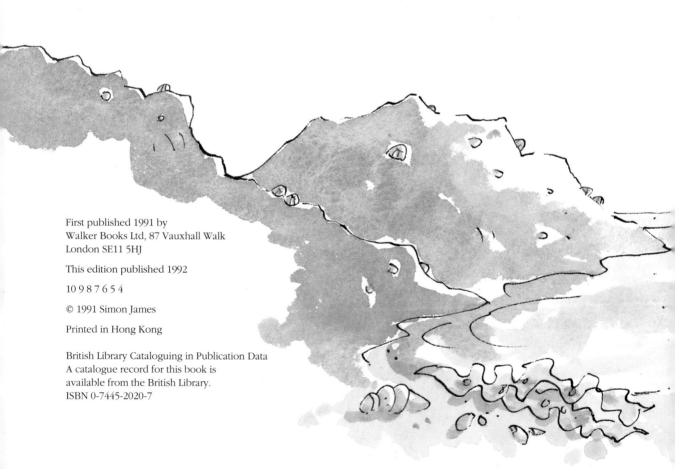

First published 1991 by
Walker Books Ltd, 87 Vauxhall Walk
London SE11 5HJ

This edition published 1992

10 9 8 7 6 5 4

© 1991 Simon James

Printed in Hong Kong

British Library Cataloguing in Publication Data
A catalogue record for this book is
available from the British Library.
ISBN 0-7445-2020-7

Sally and the Limpet

Simon James

WALKER BOOKS
AND SUBSIDIARIES
LONDON • BOSTON • SYDNEY

Not long ago, on a Sunday, Sally was down on
the beach exploring, when she found a

brightly coloured, bigger-than-usual limpet shell.
She wanted to take it home but, as she pulled,

the limpet made a little squelching noise
and held on to the rock.

The harder Sally tugged, the more tightly
the limpet held on,

until, suddenly, Sally slipped and
fell – with the limpet stuck to her finger.

Though she pulled with all her might, it just
wouldn't come off. So she ran over to her dad.

He heaved and groaned, but the limpet made a
little squelching noise and held on even tighter.

So, that afternoon, Sally went home in the car with a limpet stuck to her finger.

When they got home, her dad tried using his tools.
Her brother tried offering it lettuce and cucumber.

But, that night, Sally went to bed with a
limpet stuck to her finger.

Next day it was school.

All her friends tried to pull the limpet off her finger.
Mr Wobblyman, the nature teacher,
said that limpets
live for twenty years,
and stay all their
lives on the
same rock.

In the afternoon, Sally's mother took her
to the hospital, to see the doctor.

He tried chemicals, injections, potions and pinchers.
Sally was beginning to feel upset.

Everyone was making
too much fuss all around her.

She kicked over the doctor's chair and ran.

She ran through the endless corridors.
She just wanted to be on her own.

She ran out of the hospital and through the town.

She didn't stop when she got to the beach.

She ran through people's sandcastles.
She even ran over a fat man.

When she reached the water, she jumped in
with all her clothes on.

Sally landed with a big splash

and then just sat in the water.
The limpet, feeling at home once more,

made a little squelching noise and
wiggled off her finger.

But Sally didn't forget what Mr Wobblyman,
the nature teacher, had said.

Very carefully, she lifted the limpet
by the top of its shell.
She carried it back across
the beach, past the
fat man she had
walked on,

and gently, so gently, she put the limpet back
on the very same rock where she had found it
the day before. Then, humming to herself,

she took the long way home across the beach.

MORE WALKER PAPERBACKS
For You to Enjoy

Also by Simon James

THE WILD WOODS

Jess would like to keep a squirrel – Grandad's not so sure.
Perhaps the answer lies amongst the many wonders
to be found in the Wild Woods.

"A breath of fresh air… Witty and sparkling line-and-wash pictures…
Full of humour and vitality." *The Guardian*

0-7445-3661-8   £4.50

MY FRIEND WHALE

The moving story of a boy and the whale
with whom he plays each night. Then one sad
night the whale does not come…

"A lovely, gentle picture book with beautiful,
blue illustrations." *Practical Parenting*

0-7445-2349-4   £4.99

DEAR GREENPEACE

"One of the best books of the year, taking the form of
letters between a small girl and Greenpeace, to which she writes
for advice about a whale she finds in her garden pond…
A perfect book for 3 to 5-year-olds."
Valerie Bierman, The Scotsman

0-7445-3060-1   £4.50